This Notebook Belongs To

____

Made in the USA
Monee, IL
24 April 2022

95263058R00056